KU-004-418

He can never get the right day or the right present for that matter.

But Mr Muddle had a plan. A plan to make sure that this Christmas he would get the right day.

MR. MEN

12 Days of Christmas

Roger Hargreaves

Original concept by
Roger Hargreaves

Written and illustrated by
Adam Hargreaves

H45 827 961 2

Now, you and I know that Christmas is in the winter, in December, the 25th of December to be exact.

Mr Muddle on the other hand is not like you and I.

He does not know when Christmas is. In fact Mr Muddle has never got it right.

For instance, last year he gave Mr Lazy a football for Christmas . . . on the 25th of July. In the middle of the summer!

So on the 25th of January, Mr Muddle went to see Mr Messy.

"Happy Christmas," he announced, giving him a brand new bath. The wrong day. And the wrong present if Mr Messy was honest, but Mr Muddle had a plan and he was going to stick to it.

On the 25th of February he gave Little Miss Tiny a new pair of shoes.

The wrong day and the wrong size!

On the 25th of March he gave Mr Grumpy a joke book.

Mr Grumpy thought he must be joking.

On the 25th of April, Mr Muddle gave Little Miss Quick a pet tortoise.

"He's not very quick off the mark," observed Little Miss Quick.

On the 25th of May he gave Mr Bump a skateboard.

OUCH!

On the 25th of June he gave Mr Tickle a skipping rope.

What a tangle!

On the 25th of July he gave Little Miss Sunshine an umbrella.

I don't think she'll be needing that!

On the 25th of August, Mr Muddle gave Mr Quiet
a drum kit.

Mr Noisy was very jealous.

On the 25th of September he gave the Little Miss Twins one pair of socks.

"Oh, too kind," said the Twins.

On the 25th of October he gave Little Miss Whoops a china vase.

WHOOPS!

On the 25th of November, Mr Muddle gave Mr Slow
a sports car.

"Heeeeelp!"

Mr Muddle had been wrong eleven times. So when he got up on the 25th of December, his twelfth day of Christmas, he was sure he must have the right day.

He took a Christmas pudding round to his neighbour and knocked on his door.

"Happy Christmas!" Mr Muddle announced proudly, to his friend.

"I think you're in a muddle, Mr Muddle. It can't be Christmas because I'm off on my summer holiday!" said . . .

. . . Mr Wrong!